WHAT COLOR IS IT?

by Sheila Rivera

first step nonfiction

Lerner Publications Company · Minneapolis

The sky is blue.

This hat is red.

This fish is orange.

This bird is green.

These flowers are yellow.

These grapes are purple.

What colors do you see?